THE SECRET SOCIETY OF MONSTER HUNTERS

THE HYDRA'S VENOMOUS BLOOD

by Christina Hill

illustrated by Jared Sams

D1711998

TGP
TORCH GRAPHIC PRESS

Published in the United States of America by Cherry Lake Publishing Group
Ann Arbor, Michigan
www.cherrylakepublishing.com

Reading Adviser: Beth Walker Gambro, MS, Ed., Reading Consultant, Yorkville, IL

Book Design: Book Buddy Media

Photo Credits: page 1: ©Maisei Raman/Shutterstock; background: ©Irina-PITTORE/Shutterstock; page 7: ©Pixabay(background); page 7: ©Olena Zhdanovskykh/Shutterstock; page 7: ©Pixabay(lined paper); page 9: ©Artur Balytskyi/Shutterstock; page 15: ©Vidal 15/Shutterstock; page 19: ©Les Perysty/Shutterstock; page 30 ©Artur Balytskyi/Shutterstock

Torch Graphic Press is an imprint of Cherry Lake Publishing Group.

Library of Congress Cataloging-in-Publication Data has been filed and is available at catalog.loc.gov

Cherry Lake Publishing Group would like to acknowledge the work of the Partnership for 21st Century Learning, a Network of Battelle for Kids. Please visit http://www.battelleforkids.org/networks/p21 for more information.

Printed in the United States of America
Corporate Graphics

TABLE OF CONTENTS

Ha! I don't need to **campaign**. I'm popular!
JORGE FOR PREZ
VOTE
JORGE FOR CLASS PRESIDENT
VOTE

Sounds like someone suffers from **hubris**.
And a bit of a big head!

I am confident I can win this electio on my own!
VOTE
JORGE FOR CLASS PRESIDENT
JORGE FOR PREZ
VOTE

campaign: performing activities that will help win an election

hubris: excessive pride or self-confidence

RGE AND ELENA'S UNCLE
AN INVENTOR WHO
ILT A TIME MACHINE.
TIO
URGENT MISSION! Come quickly!
We have a mission from my **Tío** Hector. Are you in?

Let's do it!
RGE AND HIS FRIENDS ARE MONSTER HUNTERS.
EY WORK TOGETHER TO KEEP THE MAGICAL
ORLD SEPARATE FROM THE HUMAN WORLD.
Finally! That last mission was forever ago.

What do you guys
now about the hydra
rom ancient Greece?

The **civilization** of ancient Greece began in the 8th century BCE.

tío: "uncle" in Spanish

civilization: a developed culture and society belonging to a group of people

I read about the hydra when we studied Greek **mythology**.
GREEK MYTHOLOGY

Last week, an **archaeologist** dug up a vial of hydra blood. This poisonous blood could destroy hundreds of people.
NEWS
VIALS OF MYSTERIOUS BLOOD DISCOVERED
So keeping the hydra alive means no hidden vials of blood today. We're really on a mission to save the hydra!

Tío, can we really save such a huge monster?
HYDRA
We can handle anything.

Remember to work together and stay safe. You only have one day before you need to come home.

mythology: sacred stories that explain the world for a group of people; folktales

archaeologist: a person who studies human history, usually through excavation

TIPS FOR THE TIME PERIOD

* Ancient Greece was a collection of independent **city-states** that were often at war with one another.
* The **agora** was the center of activity. This is the outdoor center where people would meet, shop, and participate in politics.
* Greek theaters were also outdoors. People loved to attend festivals and plays at the theater.
* Most men worked as farmers, fishermen, educators, or soldiers. Women worked in the home.
* Children played sports and games. The Greeks invented the Olympics!
* Ancient Greeks ate a diet of bread, cheese, fish, and veggies. They ate with their hands and were known for eating meals lying on their sides!
* Religion focused on the tales of the gods and goddesses, or mythology. Greek temples were dedicated to different gods.

city-states: cities that independently govern themselves

agora: a public open space in ancient Greece

Welcome to Argos.
Let's find our hydra!

Argos is a narrow **peninsula** in southern Greece. It is one of the oldest city-states. The hydra lived at Lake Lerna, just south of Argos.

No pants?
Dude, we're wearing dresses.
Now you two know what it's like to be stuck in a dress! At least they have these cool translators to help us understand the language.

And no real shoes in all this mud? Gross.

peninsula: an area of land surrounded by water except for one piece connecting to the mainland

Men would hang out together at bath houses or government centers. Women would meet at the water wells to chat.

PACKING LIST

* Ancient Greeks rarely wore shoes. They did everything barefoot! If they needed shoes, they wore sandals.
* Everyone in ancient Greece wore a simple light-colored tunic called a **chiton**. It was held in place with a belt. Men's tunics were knee-length, and women's were ankle-length.
* The climate in Greece is mild and warm. Not much clothing was needed.
* Women wore gold and silver jewelry. They wore their long hair in braids and curls.
* Men had short, slicked-down, and parted hairstyles.
* Don't forget your **drachma** if you want to buy anything!

chiton: a gown or tunic from ancient Greece

drachma: silver coins used as currency in Greece

Where can we find this hydra? We're in the middle of a city-state.
According to mythology, the hydra was killed by the **demigod** Heracles. Let's find him.

Heracles was known as Hercules in Roman mythology.

Isn't Heracles the really strong hero who completes all those crazy tasks?
Exactly! If we can stop him from killing the hydra, we can keep the people safe from the poisonous blood.

Well, where can we find this Heracles guy?

Theater was popular in ancient Greece. The outdoor arenas were shaped like bowls. This allowed voices to be heard all the way in the back.

I remember reading about Heracles and his love of hot springs and baths. I think that's a bath up ahead!

demigod: more powerful than a human but less powerful than a god.

Did you hear? He's here!
Yes! I left in the middle of a political debate for this!

Excuse me, but who's here?
The great HERACLES!

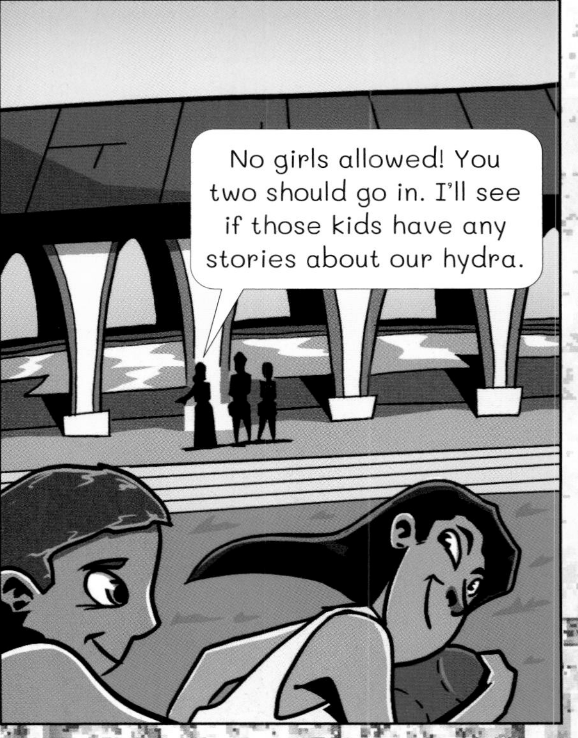
No girls allowed! You two should go in. I'll see if those kids have any stories about our hydra.

Well, my feet could use a bath! Let's go.

Cleanliness was important to the ancient Greeks, although they did not have soap. They scrubbed their bodies with blocks of clay. Then they rubbed oil into their skin.

As you all know, King Eurystheus has ordered me to complete **feats** of strength to prove myself. I just defeated a lion!

My next feat will be to kill the hydra!

He is going to kill the hydra. We need to stop him!
Let's tell him we have a special mission that only he is strong enough to complete.

Ahh, appeal to his prideful nature? Excellent plan!

feats: bold or skillful acts

Heracles, we need your help! You are the only one brave enough for this dangerous mission.
Your strength is unmatched! You are our only hope.

Dangerous missions are my specialty. But you came at a bad time. I am off to destroy the hydra.

Guys, I didn't learn much about our monster, but I had the best time playing ball. These kids are so good at sports!

Sports were popular in ancient Greece. They made balls out of inflated pigs' bladders. Greek children would paint and decorate the bladders.

You must be Heracles. Did they tell you about the hydra?
What do you know about the hydra? Are you an... **oracle**?

Oracles were valued and trusted in ancient Greece. People believed that their power to tell the future came from the gods.

Yes, I am. I am here to tell you that you must help us save the hydra—or else you will surely dieeeee.
You want me to *save* the hydra? That thing is a monster!

Trust us. We know how this story ends. If you kill the hydra, its poisonous blood will come back to haunt you. You will die by its poison.
We are saving your life. You need to let us help you.

oracle: a person whom ancient cultures believed could see the future

WHAT IS A HYDRA?

* The hydra is a gigantic snakelike monster. It has a varying number of heads. One main head is immortal.
* If you cut off 1 of the heads, 2 heads will grow back in its place. This is why the number of heads will differ.
* The hydra in ancient Greece had 9 heads.
* The hydra can spit acid, and it breathes out a deadly gas that can kill you.
* The hydra's poisonous blood is strong enough to kill a god.
* The hydra can swim.

I have faith in your oracle friend. You may join me on my journey to the hydra. I am the only one strong enough to face this monster.

Is someone going to tell him that we have faced more monsters than he has?

You may ride in my chariot. Brace yourself. We travel fast!

I think I can *run* faster than this.

Transportation was limited and roads were dirt paths. Ships were used to travel long distances. Only the wealthy could afford horses and chariots. Most people walked.

Legend says that the hydra lives in this lake. This is 1 of the entrances to the Underworld.

The ancient Greeks believed that Lake Lerna was bottomless.

Let's try and stay out of the Underworld, team.
Deal.

The Greeks believed the Underworld was where a person's soul would go after they died and separated from their physical body.

Stand back!

HISS
Watch out for the spit!

Oof!

Stop fighting it. Remember that saving this monster will save your life. Let us help you.
I never need help. I win on my own.

Working together is the only way we can win this fight.
He's right, Heracles. Let's come up with a plan.

SURVIVAL TIPS

* Cover your face. You must protect yourself from the poisonous breath.
* Do not get too close. The hydra can spit acid that will burn you.
* Remember that cutting off 1 head will make 2 grow back in its place!
* Fire may be your only chance. If you can burn the stump after cutting off a head, it may prevent new heads from growing back.
* The only way to destroy the hydra is to remove the last remaining immortal head.
* Or, try talking to the hydra. Maybe she just needs a helpful friend.

We're not here to fight you! We want to save you.

The hydra was feared by the ancient Greeks because she would **pillage** their villages.

Save me from what? The humans are afraid of me. No one comes to this lake.

pillage: to take things from a town by force

We need to save you from being killed by this guy. Saving your life will keep humans safe from your poisonous blood.
This monster does not care about humans! It destroys their villages and eats their cattle.
That's not
ue. I do care.

I only go into the village and eat their animals because I am so hungry. There is nothing left to eat here by the lake.
RRMMMBBLL

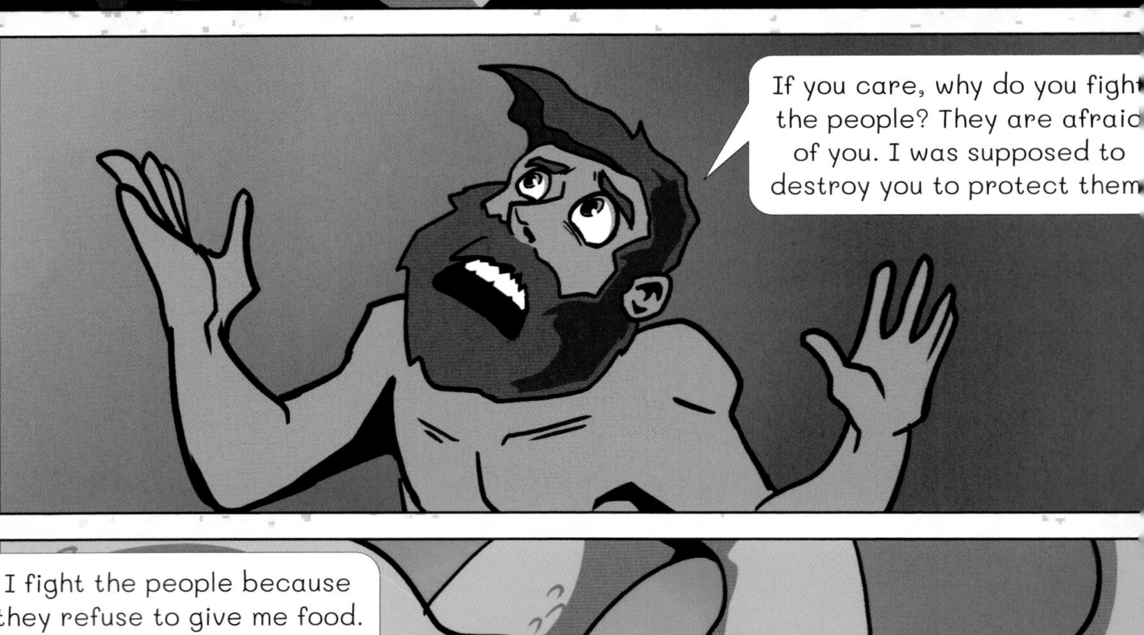
If you care, why do you figh
the people? They are afrai
of you. I was supposed to
destroy you to protect them

I fight the people because they refuse to give me food. I have no friends. Nobody will help me.

We'll help you. We can be your friends.

Let's find you a new place to live.
Good thinking. I know just the spot!

Guys, this ship has eyes.

Greek ships were known for being painted and decorated with marble eyes, 1 on each side of the ship's bow. These eyes were meant to protect the ships from harm.

Welcome, Hydra, to your new home across the lake.

Are you sure she is safe? Can you promise no humans will find her here?

I thought you were an oracle. You should know she is safe here. The humans do not dare sail their ships to this side of the lake. They are afraid of the Underworld.

Greece is a collection of islands and peninsulas. It is surrounded by 3 different seas. Sailing was the only way to travel between islands.

This place is perfect.
Thank you for your help, Heracle

No, thank you. I learned that even a demigod like me needs help sometimes.

I will never leave this paradise! Thank you for your help, friends.

Goodbye, Hydra!

So, wise oracle... what else do you see in my future?

All I can say is that you will *not* die from the poisoned hydra blood.

Stay safe, brave monster hunters.
You too, Heracles.

Ah! It feels great to be wearing pants again!

The hydra is safe now.
And we taught a demigod to ask for help when he needs it.

I sure could use your help with my election campaign.
We're already on it!

CREATE YOUR OWN MYTHOLOGY

The gods were important to the ancient Greeks. They believed that gods ruled over everything, including things like weather, education, food, and war. Many gods had special traits and talents, such as wisdom, strength, and magic powers.

Create your own modern mythological god or goddess. Keep in mind the following:

* Your god must rule over a modern idea: cell phones, video games, sports, modern dance moves, sports cars, space shuttles, and so on.
* Your god should have a unique name.
* Give your god a backstory. Describe how they were created or where they were raised.
* Describe your god's attributes. What do they look like? Do they have any special skills or powers?
* What moral can your god's story teach people?

LEARN MORE

BOOKS

Pearson, Anne. *Ancient Greece.* London, England: DK Eyewitness, 2014.

Ramenah, David, and Marios Christou. *Greek Mythology Explained.* Coral Gables, FL: Mango Publishing Group, 2018.

WEBSITES

DK Findout—Ancient Greece
https://www.dkfindout.com/us/history/ancient-greece

Ducksters—Ancient Greece for Kids
https://www.ducksters.com/history/ancient_greece.php

THE MONSTER HUNTER TEAM

JORGE

TÍO HECTOR'S NEPHEW, JORGE, LOVES MUSIC. AT 16 HE IS ONE OF THE OLDEST MONSTER HUNTERS AND LEADER OF THE GROUP.

MARCUS

MARCUS IS 14 AND IS WISE BEYOND HIS YEARS. HE IS A PROBLEM SOLVER, OFTEN GETTING THE GROUP OUT OF STICKY SITUATIONS.

Derby Devils

FIONA

FIONA IS FIERCE AND PROTECTIVE. AT 16 SHE IS A ROLLER DERBY CHAMPION AND IS ONE OF JORGE'S CLOSEST FRIENDS.

ELENA

ELENA IS JORGE'S LITTLE SISTER AND TÍO HECTOR'S NIECE. AT 14, SHE IS THE HEART AND SOUL OF THE GROUP. ELENA IS KIND, THOUGHTFUL, AND SINCERE.

AMY

AMY IS 15. SHE LOVES BOOKS AND HISTORY. AMY AND ELENA SPEND ALMOST EVERY WEEKEND TOGETHER. THEY ARE ATTACHED AT THE HIP.

TÍO HECTOR

JORGE AND ELENA'S TÍO IS THE MASTERMIND BEHIND THE MONSTER HUNTERS. HIS TIME TRAVEL MACHINE MAKES IT ALL POSSIBLE.

GLOSSARY

agora (AG-er-uh) a public open space in ancient Greece

archeologist (ahr-kee-AH-luh-jist) a person who studies human history, usually through excavation

campaign (kam-PEYN) performing activities that will help win an election

chiton (KAI-ton) a gown or tunic from ancient Greece

city-states (sit-ee stAYts) cities that independently govern themselves

civilization (sih-vuh-lai-ZEI-shuhn) a developed culture and society belonging to a group of people

demigod: (DEH-mee-gaad) a mythological person more powerful than a human but less powerful than a god.

drachma (DRAK-muh) silver coins used as currency in Greece

feats (FEETS) bold or skillful acts

hubris (HYOO-bris) excessive pride or self-confidence

mythology (mi-THAH-luh-jee) sacred stories that explain the world for a group of people; folk tales

oracle (OR-uh-kuhl) a person whom ancient cultures believed could see the future

peninsula (puh-NIN-suh-luh) an area of land surrounded by water except for one piece connecting to the mainland

pillage (PIL-ij) to take things from a town by force

tío (TEE-oh) "uncle" in Spanish

INDEX